2'

This Manuscript Belongs To

Sir/Lady

_____

To Wilf, with love – G.A.

To Sophie Harper Dennick – K.P.

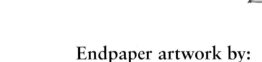

Endpaper artwork by:

Praise Ayinde, aged 7; Atinuke Obisanva-Odubanio, aged 8

Skye Mavolwane-Wright, aged 7

Reuben Baldwin, aged 7

Korky Paul would like to thank **St Saviour's Primary School, Herne Hill**
for their help with the endpapers

PUFFIN BOOKS
UK | USA | Canada | Ireland | Australia
India | New Zealand | South Africa
Puffin Books is part of the Penguin Random House group of companies
whose addresses can be found at global.penguinrandomhouse.com.
puffinbooks.com
First published 2015
001
Text copyright © Giles Andreae, 2015
Illustrations copyright © Korky Paul, 2015
The moral right of the author and illustrator has been asserted
Made and printed in China
A CIP catalogue record for this book is available from the British Library
ISBN: 978–0–723–27047–8

www.korkypaul.com

Sir Scallywag
~ and the
Battle of Stinky Bottom

Giles Andreae
and Korky Paul

PUFFIN

King Colin was a foolish man
With very little brain,
But in his ancient castle
Was a library, all the same.

He mainly kept the shelves stocked up
With doughnuts and baked beans,
But he sometimes brought in comic books
And football magazines.

His forebears, though, unlike the king,
Were men of great discerning,
Who had filled this room for many years
With wisdom, truth and learning.

One Sunday, Colin told his queen,
"Bye, diddums, toodle-oo.
The royal tum-tum's grumbling
For a little treaty-poo."

So he shuffled to the library
For a snack and a relax,
But just before the doughnut shelf
He stopped dead in his tracks.

Yes, for the first time in his life
A book had caught his eye.
It was big and old and cobwebbed.
It was dusty, dark and dry.

The spine just seemed to draw him in,
And, although he wasn't clever,
He managed to make out the title
How To Live Forever.

Intrigued, King Colin grabbed it
And began to turn the pages,
Until his wife appeared and said,
"That doughnut's taking ages!

"Good Lord!" she gasped. "Is that a book?"
"I think so," he replied.
"At least, it seems to have a lot
Of words and stuff inside.

"But listen – this is marvellous!"
He bellowed with a chortle.
"There's a giant Golden Sausage
That could make us both immortal!

"Just think how weepy you would be
If diddums went and died.
We need our finest knight for this . . .

"...Sir Scallywag!" he cried.

"I know you're only six years old,"
The king began explaining,
"But all my other knights-at-arms
Are off at knitting training.

"And, besides, they're all so hopeless
That they'd not know what to do,
And you're the prince of danger.
You're the king of daring-do!"

Sir Scallywag said, "Highness,
I am ready and I'm armed.
Now, tell me all about this quest.
Your wish is my command!"

"Ride through the forest," Colin said,
"For twenty days and nights,
Until you reach a lake that's lit
By pallid, ghostly lights.

"You'll smell it long before you're there.
It's putrid, rank and rotten,
And everybody knows it
By the name of
Stinky Bottom.

"And when the moon is high and full
You'll hear the swamp trolls sing,
And there before your eyes
You'll see the most amazing thing.

"A Golden Sausage, bright and clear,
Should rise up through mist,
And glow with a celestial light
That no one can resist.

"Retrieve that Golden Sausage,
Which will make me live forever.
It will match my underpants as well.
How's that, old bean, for clever?

"Good luck, farewell," King Colin said.
"I'm off now for a doze.
Oh, one more thing . . . I'd probably take
A clothes peg for your nose."

So brave Sir Scallywag rode out
Beyond the castle door,
And much further through the woods
Than any knight had been before.

At last he reached the forest's edge
And swiftly started choking.
"This stench is foul!" gasped Scallywag.
"I thought the king was joking!"

And, sure enough, as he looked up
He had to rub his eyes.
At least a hundred filthy trolls
Were eating swamp-slime pies.

And every troll who gobbled one
Would hiccup, cough, curse,
And then they'd do a giant belch . . .
Or something even worse!

And all the while they sang a song
About what they were eating.
Oh crikey! thought Sir Scallywag.
They're going to take some beating!

Just then the moon
broke through the clouds
And shone its silver light,
And Scallywag bore witness . . .

...to the most amazing sight.

A giant Golden Sausage
Rose atop a slender column,
And all the trolls looked on with awe,
Their faces pale and solemn.

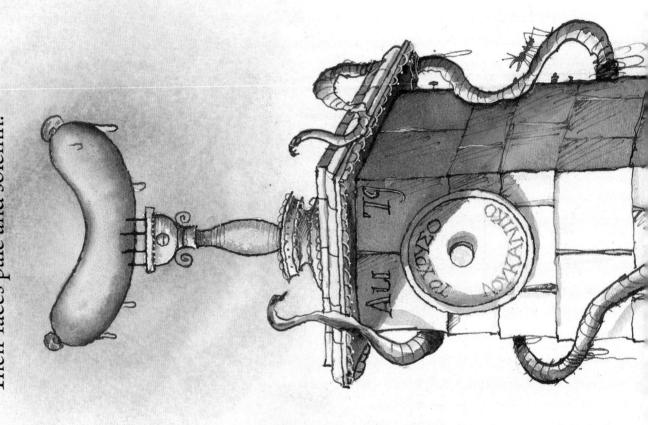

Then suddenly the king troll cried,
"Begin the dancing song!"
And all the other trolls cut loose
And sang and danced along.

"The Sausage!" said Sir Scallywag.
"That's what I've come to take!"
Then swiftly he unsheathed his sword
And strode across the lake.

"Hey, not so fast!" the king troll cried.
"What do you think you're doing?"
And in that vile and stinking lake
A battle started brewing.

Sir Scallywag fought bravely,
But he knew he was outnumbered.
There's only one of me, he thought,
And they're at least a hundred!

"But I've noticed something strange," he mused,
"About how they're behaving.
Food songs seem to make them eat,
And dance songs start them raving.

"And now they're singing fighting songs
It looks as though I'm losing.
So . . . I'm going to sing a sleeping song
And see if they start snoozing!"

The lullaby the brave knight sang
Made all the trolls feel dozy.
And, one by one, they snuggled up
And lay down, warm and cosy.

He speared the Golden Sausage,
Galloped homeward at full speed,
And appeared before the king and queen
Atop his trusty steed.

"Your Sausage!" cried Sir Scallywag.
"Oh, thank you!" sighed the queen.
"It's simply the most wondrous thing
I've ever, EVER seen!"

"Let's feast on it tonight, my dear,"
The king said to his wife.
"Oh, how I'm looking forward
To our everlasting life!"

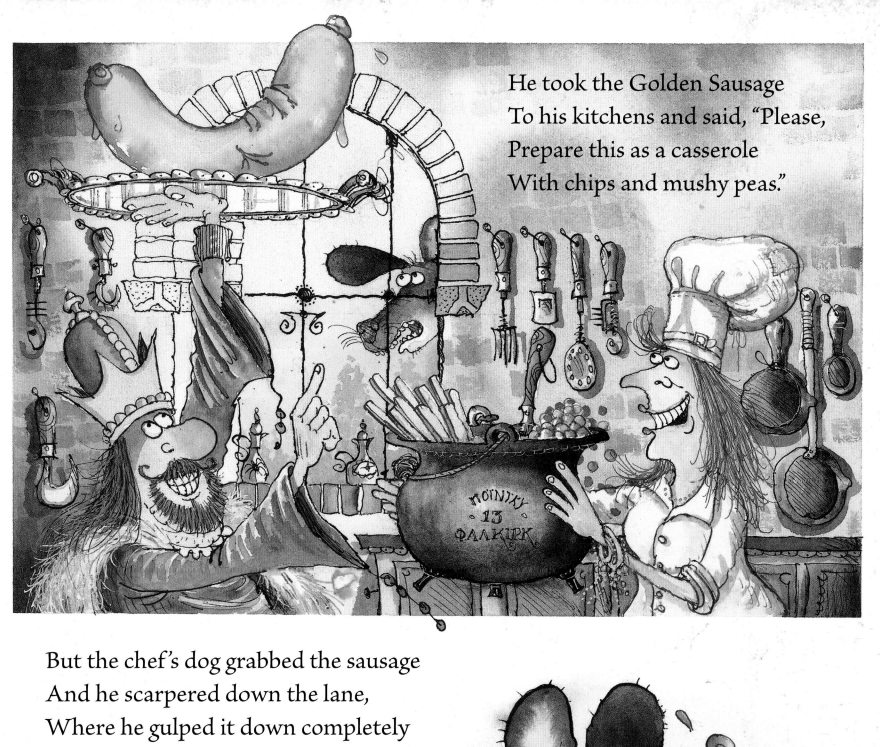

He took the Golden Sausage
To his kitchens and said, "Please,
Prepare this as a casserole
With chips and mushy peas."

But the chef's dog grabbed the sausage
And he scarpered down the lane,
Where he gulped it down completely
And was never seen again.

The dinner was still served that night
Upon the royal carpet,
But with sausages the chef had bought
From down the local market.

The king and queen knew nothing
But you still can hear them say,
"Oh, diddums, I adore you.
You look younger every day!"

And what became of that poor dog?
Yes, that's the only question.
Well, you'll find him in his bed
With everlasting indigestion!

So, you may not live forever,
Even with that sausage stew,
But for a life that's full and happy
Just be good . . .

and kind . . .

and TRUE!